Midnight Clear

Midnight
Clear

Leslie Thomas

ILLUSTRATED BY

SHIRLEY FELTS

LONDON

Arlington Books

MIDNIGHT CLEAR
first published September 1978
by Arlington Books (Publishers) Ltd
3 Clifford Street Mayfair London W1
in an edition limited to 500 copies

This edition
first published October 1978

Text © 1978 Leslie Thomas
Illustrations © 1978 Arlington Books

Printed by Ebenezer Baylis & Son Ltd
The Trinity Press, Worcester, and London

ISBN 0 85140 291 7

Midnight Clear

BY MID-MORNING ON CHRISTMAS EVE, THE EXCITEMENT within Mr. Henry Pargeter had expanded to such dimensions that he feared he might actually float from the floor of his office and end up among the balloons tethered to the ceiling.

Other people felt the same, of course; the manager was handing out cigars, Mr. Simmonds (Accounts) revealed a secret bottle of sweet sherry, the office boy was chasing the post girl, and Miss Murtagh (Underwritings) stood with annual negligence beneath the company mistletoe. Throughout the entire building, the staff were similarly expansive, as though Christmas had arrived quite unexpectedly. Desks were slammed with a bravado that suggested they would never be opened again. Mr. Pargeter shut his with the rest and then, performing a lithe, polite glide through his jovial colleagues, he made *his run for freedom.*

At noon he was at Paddington and two hours beyond that, the train whistling west, he thought he could smell the hill country. At tea time, with bursting joy, he saw the long and melancholy sea.

Mr. Pargeter was escaping from Christmas. By choice he was a singular man and Christmas caused him to be nervous. He shied from its nerve-racking cheerfulness; its frantic and gigantic eating; its induced panic and, more than anything, the crushing together of people confined in houses, private and public, with throngs of

other people, some of them relations. He had a name for
it : he called it Santa Claustrophobia. There was, however,
nothing remotely Scroogish about his attitude. He had
never said 'humbug' to anyone in his life, except possibly
to a confectioner. At the commencement of December,
he dispatched presents to all his nieces and nephews and
to a lady he once knew quite well at Bromley, and was
grateful when they knew better than to visit him or send
him gifts in return.

The previous year, at that same season, he had gone
hopefully to a small, hushed, hotel for elderly and
refined persons and had been horrified by the afternoon
antics performed in the wake (if that was the word) of the
Christmas pudding and coloured hats. A fat-legged
woman with wild eyes had actually danced upon the
table !

As soon as he decently could, he had crept out and
walked in a sooty but blessedly bare park until the
Christmas Day sun had set and he could return to his
room without being observed. But in the evening they
had made him play charades.

No, quite definitely, the season was not for him. He
liked best the day of December 27th, when the world
was a little older, when everywhere seemed grey and
vacant and exhausted. Then he really appreciated it,
walking like an echo in the solemn city, growling tugs on
the river tugging at his elderly romantic heart, and
drinking a modest beer in the stunned silence of his
local public house.

But this Christmas it was all to be changed. He almost
hugged himself in anticipation of the rare treat in prospect. What a marvellous plan he had made !

The afternoon closed about the train journeying in one

direction and the countryside journeying in the other. Fields diminished to a nicety. Lit windows blinked in amazement as they ran by. They reached Sandly-by-Sea before the shops closed.

At the station the porter had a tentative sprig of holly in his hat, but that apart it appeared mercifully unjolly. The lamps seemed to be screwing up their eyes to see through the darkness, there was a wisp of salty rain on Mr. Pargeter's appreciatively upturned face and the briny air blew in his nose and his ears, a fine sensation.

Like all seaside towns, Sandly appeared somewhat embarrassed by Christmas. It had strung its conventional coloured lights and there were Christmas trees along the front, but the channel wind, unimpressed, bounced the lights on their wires and rattled the alien firs.

To its credit, the town had dressed bravely for the part. But it was unsure of its lines. For the summer bathing huts were still lined on the beach, the pleasure boats, brought up on to the wintry shingle, gave the impression that they would like to be launched at the first bright period, and the tide sniffed inquiringly along the shore just as it did in July.

Mr. Pargeter lightly descended the hill from the railway to the sea. On impulse he took off his overcoat; then he blatantly undid his tie and put it in his pocket. Then, in a spasm of utter abandonment, HE OPENED HIS SHIRT COLLAR OVER HIS JACKET!

He knew that at the moment he reached the hibernating ice cream parlour at the foot of the hill the island would be in his view. The anticipation was so marvellous that he slowed down to make it last longer. Then he trotted the final few yards and looked out to see it. There it was! Still there! He smiled with excitement and peace.

[11]

The island lay, as if at anchor, a mile off-shore, almost merged now with the secret sea and the smoky sky. But it was still possible to follow the rise of its hump and the slopes that hurried to the landing place. There was a smudge of white where the sea tried eternally to surmount the rocks on the western side. It would never learn. An evening star, like a sailor's light, stood over it.

Mr. Pargeter strode along the seafront pavement. On the far side of the road there were shops splashing their window illuminations all over the late customers, but no one walked with him along by the beach which was coping with the everyday tide. Christmas carols creaked out of a loudspeaker outside Sandly Town Hall but the seasonless gulls screeched over them. It was almost five o'clock.

He went to the supermarket and purchased the provisions he would need, eschewing anything embellished with holly or reindeer or yo-ho-ho Santa Clauses, emerging with tinned steak and kidney, bacon, eggs, sausages, rice pudding and other commonday things. He strolled by beaming Christmas puddings and petrified fairies on the roofs of cakes with an understanding smile.

In the street, the late shoppers milled, clutching parcels in the manner of people who have saved something precious from an earthquake. For some reason they were all bent and hunched over their purchases with their collars turned up high although the Christmas evening was mild. Mr. Pargeter, open-shirted, walked tall between them.

He next visited the Sandly Home Decorators, lit white and deserted as a steppe. His entry patently

shocked the assistant who was on-his-mark and ready to close at the slightest possible excuse.

"Nearly closed, sir," the young man called, attempting to forestall him.

"But not quite, eh?" returned Mr. Pargeter affably. "I need six rolls of wallpaper, some paste, paint and brushes."

"Oh, is that all?" said the youth with doleful sarcasm.

"And a plumb line," added Mr. Pargeter firmly.

Sandly Home Decorators knew when it was beaten. The assistant sighed and helped Mr. Pargeter choose. Eventually, he packed it all in a long parcel. "Nothing else, sir?" he inquired.

Mr. Pargeter paused to give him a moment of regret and unease, then decided there was not. He put the parcel beneath his arm.

"Have a Happy Christmas, sir," said the youth following him to the door with a fixed wonderment, determined to close and lock it as soon as the man was outside. "I hope you get all the papering done."

"Oh, I shall, I shall," beamed Mr. Pargeter. "First thing on Christmas morning I shall start on the bedroom." He glanced doubtfully at his parcel. "I hope I've got enough paper."

"Plenty!" exclaimed the young man hastily reducing the shop door to a crevice. "Yards enough. If there's not . . ." His mouth was now pouting through a crack an inch wide. ". . . If there's not, come back after the owner has had his Christmas dinner and ring the side bell. I expect he'll be glad to open the shop for you."

But it was lost on the happy Mr. Pargeter. Despite his laden arms he positively skipped to the hardware store and purchased a deck chair which the amazed assistant had to unearth in the cellar. "Not much call for these just now, sir," he said as he took the money. The staff had been sharing a bottle of sherry and one lad cheekily shouted after him as he left the shop : "Don't go and get sunburned mister."

"Ah," beamed Mr. Pargeter, as though grateful for the reminder. "Indeed not. I must have a sun-umbrella also." He returned to the counter and the cheeky lad was sent grumbling to the cellar to find the sunshade.

At the chemist, he bought some sun-tan lotion and a pocket torch and, from the outfitters, a red-white-and-blue pair of bathing shorts and some open-toed sandals. How he was enjoying himself now ! How he enjoyed the expressions on the people's faces as they served him. Especially at the toy shop where he obtained his bucket and spade.

Eventually, far more laden than anyone in the excited street, he carried his deck chair, his bright umbrella and his rolls of wallpaper through the bemused shopping crowds with their hollied parcels. His rebellion pleased him so entirely that he opened his sun-umbrella in front of the bus station and twirled its extravagant stripes around in the dark afternoon air. Some people stared and some laughed, but most did not notice. They were too busy with Christmas.

He found Bertram the boatman in his cottage by the quay. Bertram spoke very little all through the summer and, it was said, he spoke even less in the winter because there were fewer topics for conversation. He made no comment on the strange cargo that he helped Mr. Pargeter to load on to the deck of his boat in the dim harbour, even though Mr. Pargeter made a great show of examining the wallpaper, opening out the deck chair and once more unfurling the sun-umbrella as they cast off

and set out on the calm Christmas sea. Eventually, when Mr. Pargeter stood up and placed the swimming shorts in an approximate position about his loins, as though judging them for size, Bertram was forced into a remark. "Looks like ye'll be the first one over on the island this summer," he mumbled.

Watching joyfully, Mr. Pargeter saw the island advance out of the dark. It seemed to grow around them as they reached the mooring and the hidden beach, disturbing indignant herring gulls and rabbits among the marram grass who confidently believed that they had the place to themselves. They unloaded the parcels on to the neglected shingle and then Bertram, promising to be back in three days, slipped off adding further silence to the silent night.

Standing on the strand, looking up and into the island, Mr. Pargeter almost shouted for happiness, but desisted in case it brought Bertram back. He carried his awkward parcels in relays up the beach path, on the return journey fondly touching the old boat winch, getting rustier with each year. When he had first gone to the island, as a boy, it was possible to turn the handle, but no more. He lit a small pocket torch to light his progress to his summer cottage, walking along the familiar row of bungalows, causing further rabbits to run in concern.

"Ahoy there," said Mr. Pargeter, addressing the front door of the cottage of that name. Then there came The Moorings, Channel View, The Crow's Nest, Poopdeck Villa, and Tidesturn, all blind and barred, stuffed with sleep and winter.

Eagerly he pushed on through the darkness until he came to Signal Cottage, his own, private, place. It

regarded his smile with wintry sadness. A whole archi-
pelago of flaking paintwork spread across the outer wall,
revealed by the random light of his pocket torch. The
corrugated roof had a rattle like a bad cough and the door
sighed when he opened it. He thought it might have been
a sigh of relief that someone had arrived, or perhaps just
weariness.

Hopefully, he stood at the step and looked at it. Ah,
yes, what a relief. It was just as he had left it in September,
colder of course, perhaps a touch of damp, but really just
the same. Even the seaweed he had left to dry was still
there.

Briskly, Mr. Pargeter lit the fire, made some strong
sweet tea and then fried up his dinner on the oil stove. The
lamps and the animations of the fire breathed life into the
room. Had Mr. Pargeter been able to countenance a
pantomime, he might have seen it as a transformation
scene. He went into the bedroom and measured it for the
wallpaper. He was pleased that he would have enough.
Tomorrow, Christmas Day, he would rise early and begin
the task.

He was eating his dinner and absorbed in reading the
country cricket scores from a six-month old iodine-
coloured newspaper he took from the sideboard, when a
furtive tap, followed by two more, the second more
furtive than the one before, touched the front door.

Mr. Pargeter's frown went before him like a warrior's
shield as he went to the door and opened it onto the salty
night. He opened it swiftly and rudely. In walked a
muddy muscovy duck which, with a quack of greeting,
waddled at once towards the fire and the food.

"Vladimir !" exclaimed Mr. Pargeter, hugely relieved
that it was not a human being and overjoyed that it was

[22]

this particular duck. "Vladimir! How marvellous to see you again, old chap! Do sit down."

The muscovy duck, its face turkey red, accepted some fried potatoes and some supermarket bread pudding. "You're a lucky fellow, Vladimir," Mr. Pargeter told him amiably. "Most men-duck relationships at this time of the year are on an entirely different basis. If they share a meal table, then it's not like this, believe me."

He neatly washed up and then sat down again to continue reading his newspaper.

"Torquay has its hottest day in forty years," he recited to the duck, which had now squatted fatly by the fire.

Vladimir appeared interested but unsurprised. "Prospect of a fine harvest," continued Mr. Pargeter. The elderly paper felt fragile in his fingers. "Bees swarm in Berkshire," he continued.

When it was late, he took a heavy damp overcoat from behind the door and went out. Vladimir took the hint quickly and followed him. The night had become chill and distinct. There was a lemon moon and a sky laden with December stars. The man and the duck walked across the springy, dark grass, over some gentle rocks and then stood together on the edge of the island. Below them, slightly glowing, was the hoop of beach where in August visitors' children built their sand castles. The sea came to it with the merest touch. There were night sounds, island birds inquiring who he was, the rustle of unsure animals, the easing of the sea, but that was all. He stood there with the duck and the stars.

Mr. Pargeter breathed it in, salt, sea and solitude. He made a brief bow in the direction of the mainland lights of Sandly-by-Sea. The moon polished the channel and, to the west, the lighthouse swung gymnastic arms. He could

[25]

see the headlights of cars wandering, apparently aimlessly, on the dark land and a tardy fishing boat was heading for Sandly Harbour and Christmas at home.

His lone state engulfed him, giving him a unique gladness. He was beyond the reach of the world and its preoccupations. He turned and smiled at the duck sitting obediently ten feet away. The light of his fire flapped in the cottage window behind him.

Full of happiness, Mr. Pargeter began to walk back. He had done it! He had actually escaped! His achievement, his gladness, his sense of peace filled him and warmed him in the sharp of midnight. Quietly, gladly, but almost absentmindedly, he began to sing:

"Good King Wenceslas looked out,
On a Feast of Stephen . . ."